I0535238

Dr. Barrère by Margaret Oliphant

Margaret Oliphant Wilson was born on April 4th, 1828 to Francis W. Wilson, a clerk, and Margaret Oliphant, at Wallyford, near Musselburgh, East Lothian.

Her youth was spent in establishing a writing style and by 1849 she had her first novel published: Passages in the Life of Mrs. Margaret Maitland.

Two years later, in 1851 Caleb Field was published and also an invitation gained to contribute to Blackwood's Magazine; the beginning of a lifelong business relationship.

In May 1852, Margaret married her cousin, Frank Wilson Oliphant. Their marriage produced six children but, tragically, three died in infancy. When her husband developed signs of the dreaded consumption (tuberculosis) they moved to Florence, and then to Rome where, sadly, he died.

Margaret was naturally devastated but was also now left without support and only her income from writing to support the family. She returned to England and took up the burden of supporting her three remaining children by her literary activity.

Her incredible and prolific work rate increased both her commercial reputation and the size of her reading audience. Tragedy struck again in January 1864 when her only remaining daughter, Maggie, died.

In 1866 she settled at Windsor to be closer to her sons, who were being educated at near-by Eton School.

For more than thirty years she pursued a varied literary career but family life continued to bring problems. Cyril Francis, her eldest son, died in 1890. The younger son, Francis, who she nicknamed 'Cecco', died in 1894.

With the last of her children now lost to her, she had little further interest in life. Her health steadily and inexorably declined.

Margaret Oliphant Wilson Oliphant died at the age of 69 in Wimbledon on 20th June 1897. She is buried in Eton beside her sons.

Index of Contents

CHAPTER I

Dr. Barrère was a young man who was beginning to make his way. In the medical profession, as in most others, this is not a very easy thing to do, and no doubt he had made some mistakes. He had given offence in his first practice to the principal person in the little town where he had set up his surgery by explaining that certain symptoms which his patient believed to mean heart disease were due solely to indigestion; and he still more deeply offended that gentleman's wife by telling her that her children were over-fed. These are follies which a more experienced medical man would never commit; but this one was young and fresh from those studies in which, more than in any other profession, things have to be called by their right names. In his next attempt he had nearly got into more serious trouble still, by his devotion to an interesting and difficult case, in which, unfortunately, the patient was a woman. From this he came out clear, with no stain on his character, as magistrates say. But for a doctor, as often for a woman, it is enough that evil has been said. The slander, though without proof, has more or less a sting, and is recollected when all the circumstances—the disproval, the clearing-up, even the facts of the case have been forgotten. He was, therefore, not without experience when he came to settle in the great town of Poolborough, which might be supposed large enough and busy enough to take no note of those village lies and tempests in a teapot. And this proved to be the case. He was young, he was clever, he was au courant of all the medical discoveries, knew everything that had been discovered by other men, and was not without little discoveries and inventions of his own. He was still young, a few years over thirty, at the age which combines the advantages of youth and of maturity, strong in mind and in body, loving work, and fearing nothing. If his previous encounters with the foolish side of humanity had diminished in some degree his faith in it, and opened his eyes to the risks which those who think no evil are apt to run in their first conflict with the stupidities and base ideas of men, he had yet not suffered enough to make him bitter, or more than wary in his dealings with the narrow and uncomprehending. He no longer felt sure of being understood, or that a true estimate of his intentions and motives was certain; but he did not go to the opposite extreme as some do, and take it for granted that his patients and their surroundings were incapable of doing him justice. He was sobered, but not embittered. He was wise enough neither to show too much interest, nor to betray too great an indifference. He listened seriously to the tale of symptoms which were nothing to anybody but their narrator, and he restrained his excitement when a matter of real importance, something delicate and critical, came under his view. Thus it was proved that he had learned his lesson. But he did not despise his fellow creatures in general, or think all alike guilty of affectation and self-regard, which showed that he had not learned that lesson with extravagance. He was kind, but not too kind. He was clever, but not so clever as to get the alarming character of an experimentalist—in short, he was in every way doing well and promising well. When the untoward accident occurred which cut short his career in Poolborough where he was universally well thought of and looked upon as a rising man.

It may be well before going further to indicate certain particulars in his antecedents which throw light upon Dr. Barrère's character and idiosyncrasies. He was of French origin, as may be perceived by his name. The name was not so distinctly French as held by his father and grandfather, who ignored the nationality, and wrote it phonetically Barraire. In their days, perhaps, a French origin was not an advantage. But in the days when Arnold Barrère was at college this prejudice had disappeared, and he was himself delighted to resort to the old orthography, and liked his friends to remember the accent which it pleased him to employ. Perhaps the keen logical tendency of his mind and disposition to carry everything out to its legitimate conclusion with a severity which the English love of compromise and accident prevents, were more important signs of his origin than even the accent over the e. Dr. Barrère for his part did not like to elude the right and logical ending either of an accent or a disease. It annoyed him even that his patient should recover in an irregular way. He liked the symptoms to follow each other in proper sequence; and the end which was foreseen and evident was that which he preferred to have occur, even when the avoidance of it, and deliverance of the sufferer were due to his own powers. Like his nation, or rather like the nation of his forefathers, he was disposed to carry out everything to its logical end. His outward man, like his mind, bore evidence of his parentage. He was about the middle height, of a light and spare figure, with a thickly-growing but short and carefully cropped black beard, his complexion rather dark but very clear, his voice somewhat high-pitched for an Englishman, with an animated manner, and a certain sympathetic action of head and hand when he talked, scarcely enough to be called gesticulation, yet more than usually accompanies English speech. He seemed, in short, to have missed the influence of the two generations of English mothers and manners which might have been supposed to subdue all peculiarities of race, and to have stepped back to the immediate succession of that Arnold Barrère who was the first to bring the name to this island. These individual features gave a certain piquancy, many people thought, to the really quite English breeding of the doctor, who had never so much as crossed the Channel, and knew little more French than was consistent with a just placing of the accents, especially upon the letter e.

It would be unnecessary to enter into full detail of how he formed acquaintance with the Surtees, and came to the degree of intimacy which soon developed into other thoughts. It is a proper thing enough in a story, though not very true to real life, to describe a young doctor as falling in love, by a sick bed, with the angel-daughter who is the best nurse and ministrant that a sick parent can have. Members of the medical profession are not more prone than other men to mingle their affections with the requirements of their profession, and probably a devoted nurse is no more the ideal of a young doctor than a good model is that of a painter. As a matter of fact, however, it was while attending Mrs. Surtees through a not very dangerous or interesting illness that Dr. Barrère made the acquaintance of Agnes. He might just as well have met her in the society which he frequented sparingly, for there was no particular difference in her sphere and his, but there were reasons why Miss Surtees went out little, less than most young women of her age. Her family was one of those which had ranked amongst the best in Poolborough in the time of their wealth, and no one could say still that their place was not with "the best people" of the town. But with a mercantile community more than any other (though also more or less in every other) wealth is necessary for the retaining of that position. Women who go afoot cannot keep up with those who have carriages and horses at their command, neither can a girl in whose house no dances, no dinners, no entertainments, are ever given, associate long on easy terms with those who are in the full tide of everything, going everywhere, and exchanging hospitalities after the lavish fashion of wealthy commercial society. And this was not the only reason that kept Agnes Surtees out of the world. There was one more urgent which was told, and one which no one named but every one understood. The first was the delicate health of her mother. Dr. Barrère was aware that there was not very much in this. He knew that had she been able to drive about as did the ladies who were so sorry for her, and clothe herself in furs and velvet, and take change of air whenever she felt disposed, there would have been little the matter with Mrs. Surtees. But he was too sensible to breathe a word on this subject. He held his tongue at first from discretion, and afterwards because he had found out for himself why it was that Mrs. Surtees' delicate health was kept before the public of Poolborough. It took him some time to make this discovery; but partly from hints of others, and partly from his own perceptions, he found it out at last.

It was that these two ladies were involved in the life of a third member of their household—a son and brother whom the "best people" in Poolborough had ceased to invite, and whose name when it was mentioned was accompanied with shakings of the head and looks of disapproval. Dr. Barrère did not ever see Jim Surtees until he had been acquainted with his mother and sister for nearly a year—not that he was absent, but only that his haunts and associates were not theirs. He was a young man who had never done well. He had been far more highly educated than was usual with the young men of Poolborough; instead of being sent into the counting-house in his youth he had been sent to Cambridge, which was all his father's pride and folly, the critics said, exempting Mrs. Surtees from blame in a manner most unusual. It was supposed that she had disapproved. She had come of a Poolborough family, in business from father to son, and knew what was necessary; but Surtees was from the country, from a poor race of county people, and was disposed to think business beneath him, or at least consider it as a mere stepping-stone to wealth. When he died so much less well off than was expected, leaving his family but poorly provided for, then was the moment when Jim Surtees might have proved what was in him, and stepped into the breach, replaced his mother and sister in their position, and restored the credit of his father's name. In that case all the old friends would have rallied around him; they would have backed him up with their credit, and given him every advantage. At such moments and in such emergencies mercantile men are at their best. No one would have refused the young man a helping hand—they would have hoisted him upon their shoulders into his father's place; they would have helped him largely, generously, manfully. Alas! Jim Surtees did then and there show what was in him. He had neither energy nor spirit nor ambition, nor any care for his father's name or his mother's comfort. He said at once that he knew nothing about business. What could he do? It was entirely out of his way. He scarcely knew what it was his father dealt in. Cotton? Yes—but what did he know about cotton, or bookkeeping, or anything? The young man was interviewed by all who knew him; he was sent for by the greatest merchants in Poolborough. What he ought to do was set before him by everybody who had any right to speak, and by a great many who had none. But nothing moved him. He knew nothing about business—he would do nothing in it. Why should he try what he could not do? And with these replies he baffled all the anxious counsellors who were so eager to convince him to the contrary. Then there were situations suggested, even provided, for him; but these were all subject to the same objections. Finally it came about that Jim Surtees did nothing. He had not been long enough at Cambridge to take his degree. He was modest about his own capacities even when pupils were suggested to him. He did not know enough to teach, he declared, till his modesty drove the anxious advisers distracted. What was to be done? Jim Surtees eluded every expedient to make him do anything. At last he dropped altogether, and the best people in Poolborough were conscious of his existence no more.

These were the circumstances of the Surtees family when Dr. Barrère made their acquaintance. He thought for some time that the two ladies lived alone, and that their withdrawal from society was somewhat absurd, based as it was on that delusion about Mrs. Surtees' health; but a little further information made him change his mind. He changed his mind about several things, modifying his first impressions as time went on. He had thought the mother one of those imaginary invalids who enjoy that gentle level of ill-health which does not involve much suffering, and which furnishes a pretty and interesting rôle for many unoccupied women; and he had thought her daughter an angelic creature, whose faith in her mother's migraines was such that she cheerfully and sweetly gave up the pleasures of her youth in order to minister to them. But as Dr. Barrère changed from a doctor into a friend; as he began to ask admittance at times when he was not called for, and when, last seal of a growing intimacy, he began to venture to knock at the door in the evening after dinner—a privilege which he pleaded for as belonging to the habits of his French ancestry (of which he knew so little)—his eyes were speedily opened to many things which a morning visitor would never have divined. The first time he did so, he perceived to his astonishment Agnes on the landing, half concealed by the turn of the staircase, eagerly looking down to see who it was; and her mother, though so little able to move about, was at the door of the little drawing-room, looking flushed and wretched, far more ill than when he had been called in to prescribe for her. For whom was it that they were looking? It could not be for himself, whom nobody had expected, whom they received with a tremulous kindness, half relieved, half reluctant. After a few such visits he began to see that the minds of these poor ladies were divided between pleasure in his society and fear to have him there. If he stayed a little longer than usual he saw that they became anxious, the mother breathless, with a desire to have him go away; and that even Agnes would accompany him down stairs with an eager alacrity as if she could not be comfortable till she had seen him out of the house. And yet they were always kind, liked him to come, looked for him, even would say a word which showed that they had noted his absence if for a week or so he did not appear; although while he was there they were ever watchful, starting at every sound, hurrying him away if he stayed beyond his time. The sight of a tall figure lurching along the street, of some one fumbling with a latch-key, of which he was sometimes conscious as he went away, was scarcely necessary at last to make him aware what it was that occasioned this anxiety. Mrs. Surtees saw love dawning in the Doctor's eyes. She would not shut out from her patient girl the chances of a happier lot; but what if the doctor should meet Jim! See him coming home sodden and stupid, or noisy and gay. As Dr. Barrère became intimate they had spoken to him of Jim. He was studying hard, he was writing, he was always busy, he was not fond of society. There were so many reasons why he should never appear. And by and by the doctor, with a great ache of pity, had learned all these excuses by heart, and penetrated their secret, and misconstrued their actions and habits no more.

Finally the doctor made the acquaintance of Jim, and to his great surprise not only liked him, but understood why the mother and sister were not always miserable, how life varied with them from day to day, and how even Mrs. Surtees was often cheerful, though never unwatchful, never at ease. Dr. Barrère thought with justice that nothing could be more miserable, more inexcusable, than the life the young man was leading. In theory fate should have put into every honest hand a whip to scourge such a good-for-nothing. And sometimes the doctor felt a righteous wrath, a desire to scourge till the blood came: but it was not so much out of moral indignation as out of an exasperated liking, an intolerable pity. What might happen in the house in those awful moments when all was silent, and everybody at rest save the mother and sister watching for Jim's return at night, neither the doctor nor any one knew. But at other moments Dr. Barrère found it impossible to resist, any more than the women did, the charm of a nature which had not lost its distinction even in the haunts where he had lost everything else. He even tried to attract and draw to himself the prodigal, entertaining visions on the subject and fancying how, if there were a man closely connected with the family, himself to wit, Arnold Barrère, and not merely women who wept and reproached and condoned and wept again, but never made a determined stand, nor struck a decisive blow, there might still be hope for Jim. It could not be said that this told as a motive in the fervour with which he offered himself to Agnes Surtees. The doctor was in love warmly and honestly, and as he made his declaration thought, as a lover ought, of nothing but Agnes. Yet when she hesitated and faltered, and after a moment broke the long silence and spoke to him openly of her brother, there was the warmth of a personal desire in the eagerness with which he met her confessions half way. "Jim is no drawback," he said eagerly—"to me none. I can help you with Jim. If you will have me there shall be no question of depriving him of any love or care. He shall have me in addition to help him to better things." "Oh," Agnes had cried, giving him both her hands in the fervour of love and trust, "God bless you, Arnold, for speaking of better things for Jim." And it was on this holy ground that their contract was made. Henceforward there were no concealments from him.

Dr. Barrère was not a man to let the grass grow under his feet. There was no reason why his marriage should be delayed. He wanted to have his wife—a possession almost indispensable, he assured Mrs.

Surtees, with a smile, to a medical man; and the mother, anxious to see one child's fate assured, and still more anxious, catching with feverish hope at the help so hopefully offered for the other, had no inclination to put obstacles in the way. The marriage day was settled, and all the preparations thereto begun, when the sudden horror which still envelopes the name of Surtees in Poolborough arose in a moment, and the following incidents occurred to Dr. Barrère.

CHAPTER II

He was going to visit a patient in a suburb one dark October night. But it could scarcely be called dark. There was a pallid moon somewhere among the clouds whitening the heavy mist that lay over the half-built environs of the town—dismal blank spaces—fields which were no longer fields, streets which were not yet streets. The atmosphere was charged with vapour, which in its turn was made into a dim, confusing whiteness by the hidden moon. Everybody knows how dismal are these outskirts of a great city. A house built here and there stood out with a sinister solidity against the blank around. New roads and streets laid out with indications of pavement, cut across the ravaged fields. Here and there was a mass of bricks, and there a pool of water. A piece of ragged hedgerow, a remnant of its earlier state, still bordered the highway here and there; a forlorn tree shedding its leaves at every breath of air stood at the corner where two ways met. Dr. Barrère was no ways timid, but he felt a chill of isolation and something like danger as he pushed his way towards one of the furthest points of the uncompleted road, where one house stood shivering in the vague damp and whiteness. He had to cross the other branching road, at the corner of which stood the shivering poplar, which shed its leaves as if with a perpetual shrinking of fear. There he was vaguely aware of something standing in the shade of the ragged hedgerow—a figure which moved as he passed, and seemed to make a step forward as if awaiting some one. To say that it was a figure he saw would be too distinct—he saw a movement, a something more solid than the mist, which detached itself as if with a suggestion of watchfulness, and immediately subsided again back into the shadows. Dr. Barrère, though he was not timid, felt the thrill as of a possible danger, the suggestion having something in it more moving than a distincter peril. But if there was a man lurking there waiting for some passer-by, it was not at least for him, and he walked quickly on, and presently in the interest of his patient, and in the many thoughts that hurry through every active brain, forgot the curious hint of mystery and danger which had for a moment excited his imagination.

When he approached the spot again on his return, even the suggestion had died out of his mind. His eyesight and all his faculties were keen, as befits his profession, and he saw, without being aware that he was seeing, everything that came within his range of vision. Accordingly he perceived without paying any attention, the vague figure of a man crossing the opening of the road where the poplar marked the corner, coming towards him. He saw the solid speck in the white mist approaching—then in a moment, in the twinkling of an eye, this vague silhouette in the night became a sudden swift scene of pantomimic tragedy, all done and over in a moment. A sudden movement took place in the scene; another something, almost less than a shadow, suddenly came into it from behind the poplar. No, these words are too strong. What came into the night was the sound of a crashing blow and a fall, and another figure, in a different position, standing over something prostrate, raining down, as in a fit of frantic passion, blow on blow. Passion, murder, horror, came in a second into the still confusion of the misty air. Then, swift as the sudden commotion, came a pause—a wild cry of consternation, as if for the first time the actor in this terrible momentary tragedy had become aware of what he was doing. The spectator's senses were so absorbed in the suddenness of the catastrophe that there was time enough for the whole drama to enact itself before he found voice. He had broken mechanically into a run, and thought that he called out. But it was not (it seemed to him in the hurried progression of ideas) his cry or the sound of his approach, but a sudden horror which had seized the man (was he a murderer?), who had in a moment come to himself. When the doctor at full speed, and calling out mechanically, automatically, for Help! help! reached the spot where the prostrate figure was lying, the other had taken flight down the cross road and was already invisible in the distance. The doctor's first care was for the victim. He was not an avenger of blood, but a healer of men.

Presently there appeared around him two or three startled people—one from the nearest house carrying a small lamp, which made the strangest, weird appearance in the misty night; a passer-by on his way home; a vagrant from the deserted fields. They helped the doctor to turn over the murdered man, who was still living, but no more, and who, it was evident to Dr. Barrère's experienced eyes, was on the point of death and beyond all human help. The lamp had been placed on the ground close by, and sent up an odour of paraffin along with the yellow rays that proceeded from its globe of light, and the figures kneeling and bending over the inanimate thing in the midst looked more like a group of murderers than people bringing help and succour. Some time had elapsed before the means of transporting him even to the nearest house had been procured, and by that time there was no longer any question of what could be done on his behalf, and all that was possible was to carry away the body. Dr. Barrère walked beside the melancholy convoy to the nearest police station, where he made his deposition; and then he went home in all the tremor of excitement and mental commotion. He had fortunately no visits to pay that evening of any importance; but he was too much stirred and troubled to remain quietly at home, and after a while hurried out to Agnes, his natural confidant, to tell her all about the shock he had received. It struck him with surprise to see, when he entered the little drawing-room, that Jim was with his mother and sister. It was a thing that had very seldom happened before. He sat apart from them at the writing-table, where he was writing, or making believe to write, letters. The sight of him struck Dr. Barrère with a certain surprise, but he could not have told why. There was no reason why he should not be found in his mother's drawing-room. It was true that he was rarely to be seen there, but yet sometimes he would make his appearance. This evening he had dressed for dinner, which was still more unusual: perhaps he was going out to some late evening party; perhaps some one had been expected to dinner. These thoughts flew vaguely through Dr. Barrère's mind, he could not have told why. There was no particular reason why he should thus desire to penetrate the motives of Jim Surtees' behaviour, or to explain to himself why the young man was there. The speculation passed through his head without thought, if such an expression may be used, without any volition of his, as half our thoughts do, like the chance flight of birds or butterflies across the air. They did not detain him a moment as he came forward with his greetings, and met the pleased surprise of the reception which the ladies gave him, "I thought it was too late to look for you," his Agnes said, with a brightening of all the soft lines of her face, as if the sun had risen upon a landscape. And then, as it was cold, a chair was drawn for him near the fire. "You have been kept late on your round to-night," said Mrs. Surtees. "Have you any very anxious case?"

"It is no case that has kept me," said the doctor. "I have had a dreadful encounter in the road. You know that district up beyond St. George's-in-the-fields—those half-built, desolate villas and cottages. The roads are as lonely as if they were in the middle of a wood. A new quarter by night is as bad as a bare moor."

Agnes stood listening with her hand on the back of his chair, but still a smile upon her face—the smile of pleasure at his coming. Mrs. Surtees had let her knitting fall upon her lap, and was looking at him, listening with pleased interest. They had not perceived the agitation which, indeed, until he began to speak, he had managed to suppress. "And what happened?" Mrs. Surtees said.

"I have been," he answered, his voice breaking in spite of himself, "the witness of a murder."

"Good heavens!" The ladies were too much startled to put another question except with their eager eyes. They drew closer to him; the hand of Agnes glided to his shoulder from the back of his chair. What she thought first was that his emotion did honour to him.

Then he described to them briefly what he had seen—the lurking figure in the shadow which had alarmed himself as he passed first, but which he soon perceived had no hostile intentions towards him; the appearance of the man approaching from the opposite direction as he returned; the sudden assault; the rapid, breathless, horrible suddenness of the tragedy. The ladies hung upon his lips, making exclamations of horror. It was not till afterwards that Dr. Barrère became aware that the young man at the table behind made no sign, said not a word. He had told everything, and answered half a dozen hurried, faltering questions before Jim made any remark. Then he suddenly stirred behind backs (the group at the fireside having forgotten his presence) and asked, "What are you talking about? What's happened?" in a deep, half growling voice, as of a man disturbed in his occupation by some fuss of which he did not grasp the meaning.

"Oh," said Mrs. Surtees wiping her moist eyes, "did you not hear, Jim? The doctor has seen a murder committed. God preserve us! I feel as if I had seen it myself. A dreadful thing like that coming so near us! It is as if we were mixed up in it," she said.

"A murder? Are you sure it was a murder? It might be nothing more than a quarrel—how could you tell in the dark?" said Jim, always in the same gruff, almost indignant voice.

"If you had seen it as I did you would have been in no doubt," said Dr. Barrère, turning half round, and catching a side view of the tall figure slouching with hands in his pockets, his face clouded with a scowl of displeasure, his shoulders up to his ears. This silhouette against the light gave him a thrill, he scarcely knew why. He paused for a moment, and then added, "After all you may be right; it was murder to all intents and purpose—but whether it was intended to be so there may be a doubt."

"You are always so ready to come to tragical conclusions," said Jim in easier tones. "I dare say it will turn out to have been a quarrel, and no more."

"A quarrel in which one is killed is apt to look like murder."

These words gave them all a shivering sensation. Even Jim's shoulders went up to his ears as if he shared the involuntary shudder—and Mrs. Surtees said again, drying her eyes, "It is as if we were mixed up in it. Poor man, poor man, cut off in a moment, without a thought!"

"It appears that he is a well known and very bad character," said Dr. Barrère. "I feel almost more sorry for the poor wretch that did it. The cry he gave when he saw what he had done still rings in my ears."

"Then you think he did not mean it, Arnold?"

"God knows! You would have said he meant everything that passion and rage could mean to see the blows; but that cry—"

"He repented, perhaps—when it was too late."

"It was horror—it was consternation. It was the cry of a man who suddenly saw what he had done."

There was a pause of sympathetic horror and pity. Then Jim Surtees went back to the writing-table, and Dr. Barrère continued his conversation with the ladies, which, however they tried to break into other and happier subjects, returned again and again to the terrible scene from which he had just come. They spoke in low tones together over the fire—the doctor recounting over and over again the feelings with which he had contemplated the extraordinary, sudden tragedy, the rapidity with which all its incidents followed each other, leaving him scarcely time to cry out before all was over. He was naturally full of it, and could speak of nothing else, and his betrothed and her mother, always sympathetic, threw themselves entirely into the excitement which still possessed him. It was late when he rose to go away, soothed and calmed, and with a sense of having at last exhausted the incident. It startled him as he turned round, after taking leave of Mrs. Surtees, to see that Jim was still there. And the aspect of the young man was sufficiently remarkable. The candles on the writing-table behind which he sat had burned low. They had escaped from the little red shades which had been placed over them, and were flaring low, like a level sun in the evening, upon the figure behind, which, with his head bowed in his hands and shoulders up to his ears, seemed unconscious of all that was passing. Jim neither saw nor heard the doctor move. He was absorbed in some all-important matter of his own.

Next day Dr. Barrère was still deeply occupied by the scene he had seen. He was summoned for the coroner's inquest, and he was, as was natural, questioned by everybody he met upon a subject which was in all men's mouths. It was equally natural that he should return next evening to bring the account of all the encounters he had gone through and all that was news on the subject to Agnes and her mother. Once more he noted with surprise that Jim was in the drawing-room. Was he turning over a new leaf? Had he seen the folly of his ways at last?

They were sitting as before over the fire, Dr. Barrère telling his story, the ladies listening with absorbed attention. The interest of this terrible tragedy which had taken place almost within their kin, which they were seeing through his eyes, was absorbing to them. They wanted to know everything, the most minute details, what questions had been asked him, and what he had replied. Jim was still behind backs at the writing-table with the two candles in their red shades, which did not betray his face, but threw a strange light upon his hands and the occupation in which he seemed to be absorbed. He was playing an old-fashioned game with small colored glass balls on a round board, called solitaire in the days when it was in fashion. The little tinkle of the balls as he placed them in the necessary order came in during the pauses in the talk like a faint accompaniment. But no one looked at him: they were too much absorbed in Dr. Barrère's report.

"And are you the only witness, Arnold?" Agnes asked.

"The only one who saw the deed done," he said. "It is very rarely that there is even one witness to the actual fact of a murder. But there is other evidence than mine; the man is supposed to have been seen by various people, and there is a dumb witness of the first importance, the stick which he must have thrown away, or which dropped from his hand in the horror, as I shall always believe of his discovery of what he had done."

At this point there was a ring as of the glass balls all tinkling together on the board. The doctor turned round, slightly startled in the high tension of his nerves, and saw that Jim had upset his plaything, and that the balls were rolling about the table. But this was far from being an unusual accident in the game, and neither Mrs. Surtees nor Agnes took any notice, their nerves were not strained as Dr. Barrère's had been. The mother spoke low with a natural thrill of horror and pity. "And is it known," she said, "is it known to whom the stick belongs?"

Before Dr. Barrère could reply there came a knock to the door—a knock not at the door of the room in which they sat, but below at the street door, a thing unusual indeed at that hour, but not so startling in general as to excite or alarm them.

But perhaps all their nerves were affected more or less. It was very sudden and sharp, and came into the calm domestic atmosphere with a scarcely comprehensible shock. They all turned round, and Jim, the doctor saw, had suddenly risen up, and stood with his face turned towards the door. The summons rang through the silence with an effect altogether out of keeping with its simplicity.

"Who can that be so late," said Mrs. Surtees. "Jim, will you go and see?"

"It must be some one for me," the doctor said.

"Poor Arnold! I hope it is someone near," said Agnes faltering—for neither of them believed what they said. It was something terrible, something novel, some startling new event whatever it was. Jim, instead of doing as his mother wished, sat down again behind the writing-table, within the shelter of the red shades on the candles, and they all waited, scarcely venturing to draw breath. Presently the neat parlor-maid, pale, too, and with a visible tremor, opened the door. She said, with a troubled look at her mistress, that, "Please, there was some one down stairs who wanted to speak to Mr. Jim." Mrs. Surtees was the last to be moved by the general agitation. She said, "For Mr. Jim? But let him come up, Ellen. Jim, you had better ask your friend to come upstairs."

Once more there was a terrible, incomprehensible pause. Jim, who had fallen rather than re-seated himself on the sofa which stood behind the writing-table, said not a word; his face was not visible behind the shaded lights. Mrs. Surtees threw a glance round her—a troubled appeal for she knew not what enlightenment. Then she said breathlessly, "What has happened? What is the matter? Who is it? Ellen, you will show the gentleman up stairs."

Heavens! How they stood listening, panic stricken, not knowing what they were afraid of, nor what there was to fear. Mrs. Surtees still kept her seat tremulously, and Jim, lost in the corner of the sofa, suddenly extinguished the candles—an act which they all seemed to approve and understand without knowing why. And then there came a heavy foot ascending the stairs. Mrs. Surtees did not know the man who came in—a tall soldierly man with a clear and healthful countenance. It even gave her a momentary sensation of comfort to see that Jim's "friend" was no blear-eyed young rake, but a person so respectable. She rose to meet him with her old-fashioned courtesy. "Though I have not the pleasure of knowing you," she said with a smile, which was tremulous by reason of that causeless agitation, "my son's friends are always welcome." Oh heaven above! her son's friend! Dr. Barrère was the only one among them who knew the man. The sight of him cleared the whole matter in a moment, and shed a horrible light over everything to the doctor's eyes. He made a sudden sign to the newcomer imploring silence.

"I know this gentleman, too, Mrs. Surtees," he said, "he is one of my—friends, also. Would it be taking a great liberty if I were to ask you to leave us for a few minutes the use of this room? Agnes, it is a great intrusion—but—for God's sake take her away!" he said in his betrothed's ear.

Mrs. Surtees looked at him with some surprise and an air of gentle dignity not entirely without offence. "My dear," she said to Agnes, "Dr. Barrère would not ask such a thing without good reasons for it, so let us go." She was not a woman who had been accustomed to take the lead even in her own family, and she was glad, glad beyond description, to believe that the business, whatever it was, was Dr. Barrère's business, and not—anything else. She accepted it with a trembling sense of relief, yet a feeling that the doctor was perhaps taking a little too much upon him, turning her out of her own room.

The two men stood looking at each other as the ladies went away, with Jim still huddled in the corner of the sofa, in the shade, making no sign. Dr. Barrère saw, however, that the stranger, with a glance round of keen, much-practised eyes, had at once seen him, and placed himself between Jim and the door. When the ladies had disappeared the doctor spoke quickly. "Well," he said, "what is it, Morton? Some new information?"

"Something I regret as much as any one can, Dr. Barrère. I have to ask Mr. Surtees to come with me. There need be no exposure for the moment: but I must take him without delay."

"Take him!" The doctor made a last effort to appear not to perceive. He said, "Have you too seen something, then? Have you further evidence to give, Jim?"

There was no reply. Neither did the superintendent say a word. They stood all three silent. Jim had risen up; his limbs seemed unable to support him. He stood leaning on the table, looking out blankly over the two extinguished candles and their red shades. The officer went up and laid his hand lightly upon the young man's shoulder. "Come," he said, "you know what I'm here for: and I'm sorry, very sorry for you, Mr. Jim: but no doubt you'll be able to make it all clear."

"Barrère," said Jim, struggling against the dryness in his throat, "you can prove that I have not been out of the house—that I was at home all last night. I couldn't—I couldn't, you know, be in two places at one time—could I, Barrère?"

"Mr. Jim, you must remember that whatever you say now will tell against you at the trial. I take you to witness, doctor, that I haven't even told him what it was for."

Jim ground out an oath from between his clenched teeth. "Do I need to ask?" he said. "Doesn't everybody know I hated him—and good reason too—hated him and threatened him—but, God help me, not to kill him!" cried the young man with a voice of despair.

CHAPTER III

Dr Barrèrewas left to break the news to the mother and daughter. He never knew how he accomplished this dreadful office. They came back when they heard the door shut, evidently not expecting to find him, believing that he had withdrawn with his "friend"—and the anxious, searching eyes with which his Agnes looked around the room, the mingled terror and pleasure of her look on discovering him, never faded from his mind. Mrs. Surtees was more disappointed than pleased. She said, with an evident sudden awakening of anxiety, "Where is Jim?" And then he had to tell them. How did he find words to do it? But the wonderful thing, the dreadful thing, was that after the shock of the first intimation there seemed little surprise in the looks of these poor ladies. The mother sank down in her chair and hid her face in her hands, and Agnes stood behind her mother, throwing her arms round her, pressing that bowed head against her breast. They did not cry out indignantly that it was not—could not be true. They were silent, like those upon whom something long looked for had come at last. The doctor left them after a while with a chill in his very soul. He could say nothing; he could not attempt to console them in the awful silence which seemed to have fallen upon them. Agnes tried to smile as he went away—tried with her trembling lips to say something. But she could not conceal from him that she wished him to go, that he could give no comfort, that the best thing he could do for them in their misery was to leave them alone. He went home very miserable in that consciousness of being put aside, and allowed no share in the anguish of the woman whom he loved. It was intolerable to him; it was unjust. He said to himself as he walked along that the tacit abandonment of Jim, the absence of all protest on their part that his guilt was impossible—a protest which surely a mother and sister in any circumstances ought to have made—was hard, was unjust. If all the world condemned him, yet they should not have condemned him. He took Jim's part hotly, feeling that he was a fellow sufferer. Even were he dissipated and reckless, poor fellow, there was a long, long way between that and murder. Murder! There was nothing in Jim which could make it possible that he could have to do with a murder. If he was hasty in temper, poor fellow, his nature was sweet, notwithstanding all his errors. Even he, Arnold Barrère, a man contemptuous of the manner of folly which had ruined Jim, a man with whom wrath and revenge might have awakened more sympathy—even he had come to have a tenderness for the erring young man. And to think that Jim could have lain in wait for any one, could have taken a man at a disadvantage, was, he declared to himself with indignation, impossible. It was impossible! though the two women who were nearest to him—his mother and his sister—did not say so, did not stand up in vindication of the unhappy youth.

When he had exhausted this natural indignation Dr. Barrère began to contemplate the situation more calmly, and to arrange its incidents in his mind. The horror of the thought that he was himself the chief witness affected him little at first, for it was to the fact only that he could speak, and the culprit, so far as he was concerned, was without identity, a shadow in the night, and no more. But a chill came over that flush of indignant partisanship with which he had made a mental stand for Jim when the other circumstances flashed upon him. He remembered his own surprise to find Jim in the drawing-room when he arrived at Mrs. Surtees' house; to see his dress so unusual, though scarcely more unusual than the fact of his being there. He remembered how the young man held aloof, how the candles had flared upon him neglected. The little scene came before Dr. Barrère like a picture—the candle shades standing up in a ludicrous neglect, the light flaring under them upon Jim's face. And then again, to-night: the senseless game with which he seemed to amuse himself; the tremble of his hands over the plaything; his absence of interest in the matter which was so exciting to the others. Why was Jim there at all? Why did he ask no question? Why keep behind unexcited, unsurprised, while the doctor told his story? And then the reason thrust itself upon him in Jim's own words—"I couldn't be in two places at once, could I? You can prove that I was here last night." Good God, what did it mean? Jim—Jim!—and his mother and sister, who had sunk into despair without a word, who had never said as women ought, "We know him better; it is not true—it is not true."

Dr. Barrère went home more wretched than words can say. Hard and terrible is an unjust accusation; but oh, how easy, how sweet, how possible, is even the shame which is undeserved! A century of that is as nothing in comparison with a day or hour of that which is merited—of the horror which is true. He tried to hope still that it was not true; but he felt coming over him like a pall, the terror which he could now perceive had quenched the very hearts in the bosoms of the two women who were Jim's natural defenders. They had not been able to say a word—and neither could he. Dr. Barrère stood still in the middle of the dark street with the damp wind blowing in his face as all this came before him. A solitary passer-by looked round surprised, and looked again, thinking the man was mad. He saw in a moment as by a revelation, all that was before them—and himself. The horrible notoriety, the disgrace, the endless stigma. It would crush them and tear their lives asunder: but for him also, would not that be ruin too?

CHAPTER IV

The trial took place after a considerable interval, for the assizes were just over when the man was killed. In that dreadful time of suspense and misery proof after proof accumulated slowly with a gradual drawing together as of the very web of fate. The stick which was found by the body of the murdered man was Jim's stick, with his initials upon it, in a silver band—alas, his mother's gift. He was proved to have had a desperate quarrel with the man, who was one of those who had corrupted and misled him. Then the alibi which had seemed at first so strong disappeared into worse than nothing when examined: for Jim had been seen on his flight home; he had been seen to enter furtively and noiselessly into his mother's house, though the servants were ready to swear that he had not gone out that night; and all the precautions he had taken, instead of bringing him safety, only made his position worse, being shown to be precautions consciously taken against a danger foreseen. All these things grew into certainty before the trial; so that it was all a foregone conclusion in the minds of the townspeople, some of whom yielded to the conviction with heartfelt pity, and some with an eager improving of the situation, pointing out to what horrible conclusions vice was sure to come.

Meanwhile this strange and horrible event, which had held the town for more than nine days in wonder and perturbation, and which had given a moral to many a tale, and point to many a sermon, held one little circle of unhappy creatures as in a ring of iron—unable to get away from it, unable to forget it, their hearts, their hopes, their life itself, marked forever with its trace of blood. The two ladies had roused themselves from their first stupor into a half fictitious adoption of their natural rôle as defenders of Jim. God knows through how many shocks and horrors of discovery Jim had led them, making something new, something worse, always the thing to be expected, before they had come to that pitch that their hearts had no power to make any protest at all. But when the morning rose upon their troubled souls they began to say to each other that it could not be true. It could not be true! Jim had now and then an accès of sudden rage, but he was the kind of man of whom it is said that he would not hurt a fly. How could it be possible that he would do a murder? It was not possible; any other kind of evil thing—but not that, oh, not that! They said this to each other when they rose up from the uneasy bed in which mother and daughter had lain down together, not able to separate from each other—though those rules of use and wont which are so strong on women made them lie down as if to sleep, where no sleep was. But when the light came—that awful light which brings back common life to us on the morning after a great calamity—they looked into each other's pale faces, and with one voice said, "Oh no, no, it cannot be!" "Mother," cried Agnes, "he would not hurt a fly. Oh, how kind he was when I was ill, when you had your accident—do you remember?" Who does not know what these words are—Do you remember? All that he was who is dead; all that he might have been who is lost; all the hopes, the happy prospects, the cheerful days before trouble came. No words more poignant can be said. They did not need to ask each other what they remembered—that was enough. They clasped each other, and kissed with trembling lips, and then Agnes rose, bidding her mother rest, and went to fetch her the woman's cordial, the cup of tea—which is so often all one poor female creature can offer to another by way of help.

No, no, he could not have done it! They took a little comfort for the moment. And another strange comfort they took in a thing which was one of the most damning pieces of evidence against Jim: which was that he had quarreled violently with the murdered man and denounced him, and declared hatred and everlasting enmity against him. The story of the quarrel as it was told to them brought tears, which were almost tears of joy, to Mrs. Surtees' eyes. The man who had been killed was one of those adventurers who haunt the outskirts of society wherever there are victims to be found. He had preyed upon the lives and souls of young men in Poolborough since the days when Jim Surtees was an innocent and credulous boy. It was not this man's fault that Jim had gone astray, for Jim, alas, was all ready for his fall, and eager after everything that was forbidden; but in the fits of remorse and misery which sometimes came upon him it was perhaps no wonder if he laid it at Langton's door; and that the mother should have held Langton responsible, who could wonder? The facts of the quarrel were as so many nails in Jim's coffin: but God help the poor woman, they gave consolation to his mother's heart. They meant repentance, she thought, they meant generosity and a pathetic indignation, and more, they meant succour; for the quarrel had arisen over an unfortunate youth whom the blackleg was throwing his toils around as he had thrown them around Jim, and whom Mrs. Surtees believed Jim had saved by exposing the villain. The story was told reluctantly, delicately, to the poor ladies, as almost sealing Jim's fate: and to the consternation of the narrator, who was struck dumb, and could only stare at them in a kind of stupor of astonishment, they looked at each other and broke forth into cries at first inarticulate which were almost cries of joy. "You do not see the bearing of it, I fear," said the solicitor who had the management of the case, as soon as out of his astonishment he had recovered his voice. "Oh sir," cried Mrs. Surtees, "what I see is this, that my boy has saved another poor woman's son, God bless him! and that will not be forgotten, that will not be forgotten!" This gentleman withdrew in a state of speechless consternation. "No, it will not be forgotten," he said to Dr. Barrère. "I think the poor lady has gone out of her senses, and little wonder. It is a piece of evidence which we can never get over." Dr. Barrère shook his head, not understanding the women much better than the lawyer did. This gave them consolation, and yet it was the seal of Jim's fate.

Dr. Barrère himself in the long period of waiting was a most unhappy man. He stood by the Surtees nobly, everybody said. No son could have been more attentive than he was to the poor mother who was entirely broken by this blow, and had suddenly become an old woman. And he never wavered in his faith and loyalty to Agnes, who but for that noble fidelity would, everybody said, have been the most of all to be pitied. For Agnes was young, and had all her life before her, with the stain of this crime upon her name; and if her lover had not stood by her what would have become of her? The people who had been doubtful of Dr. Barrère, as half a Frenchman, as too great a theorist, as a man who had not been quite successful in his outset, began now to look upon him with increased respect, and his firmness, his high honour, his disinterestedness were commented upon on all sides. But in his heart the doctor was far from happy. His life, too, seemed in question as well as Jim's. If the worst came to the worst, he asked himself, would society, however sympathetic for the moment, receive the family of a man who had been hanged—horrible words!—without prejudice? Would there not be a stigma upon the name of Surtees, and even upon the name of him who had given his own as a shield to the family of the murderer? He did his duty—no man more truly. He loved his Agnes with all the warmth of an honest heart, taking his share of all her trouble, supporting her through everything, making himself for her sake the brother of a criminal, and one of the objects of popular curiosity and pity. All this he did from day to day, and went on doing it: but still there were struggles and dreadful misgivings in Dr. Barrère's heart. He was a proud man, and except for what he made by his profession a poor one. If that failed him he had nothing else to fall back upon, and he already knew the misery of unsuccess. He knew what it was to see his practice wasting away, to see his former patients pass by shamefacedly, conscious of having transferred their ailments and themselves to other hands, to be put aside for no expressed reason out of the tide of life. At Poolborough he had begun to forget the experiences of his beginning, and to feel that at last he had got hold of the thread which would lead him if not to fortune, at least to comfort and the certainties of an established course of living. Would this last? he asked himself. Would it make no difference to him if he identified himself with ruin—ruin so hideous and complete? The question was a terrible one, and brought the sweat to his brow when in chance moments, between his visits and his cases, between the occupations and thoughts which absorbed him, now and then, suddenly, in spite of all the pains he took, it would start up and look him in the face. "He had a brother who was hanged," that was what people would say; they would not even after a little lapse of time pause to recollect that it was his wife's brother. The brand would go with them wherever he went. "You remember the great murder case in Poolborough? Well, these were the people, and the brother was hanged." These words seemed to detach themselves and float in the air. He said them to himself sometimes, or rather they were said in his ear, without anything else to connect them. The phrase seemed already a common phrase which any one might use—"The brother was hanged." And then cold drops of moisture would come out upon his forehead. And all the possibilities of life, the success which is dear to a man, the advancement of which he knew himself capable—was it all to go? Was he to be driven back once more to that everlasting re-commencement which makes the heart of a man sick?

These thoughts accompanied Dr. Barrère as he went and came, a son, and more than a son, to Mrs. Surtees, and to Agnes the most faithful, the most sympathetic of lovers. At such a moment, and in face of the awful catastrophe which had come upon them, any talk of marriage would have been out of place. He had, indeed, suggested it at first in mingled alarm and desperation, and true desire to do his best, in the first impulse of overwhelming sympathy, and at the same time in the first glimpse of all that might follow, and sickening horror of self-distrust lest his resolution might give way. He would have fled from himself, from all risks of this nature into the safety of a bond which he could not break. But Agnes had silently negatived the proposal with a shake of her head and a smile of pathetic tenderness. She, too, had thoughts of the future, of which she breathed no word to any one, not even to her mother. All that was in his mind as subject of alarm and misgiving was reflected, with that double clearness and vivification which is given to everything reflected in the clear flowing of a river, in the mind of Agnes. She saw all with the distinctness of one to whom the sacrifice of herself was nothing when compared with the welfare of those she loved. He was afraid lest these alarms might bring him into temptation, and the temptation be above his strength; and his soul was disturbed and made miserable. But to Agnes the matter took another aspect. All that he foresaw she foresaw, but the thought brought neither disturbance nor fear. It brought the exaltation of a great purpose—the solemn joy of approaching martyrdom. Arnold should never suffer for her. It was she who would have the better part and suffer for him.

The dreadful fact that it was Dr. Barrère only who had witnessed the murder, and that he would have to speak and prove what he had seen, became more and more apparent to them all as the time drew on. His description of the blows that had been rained down wildly on the victim, and of the lurking figure in the shadow whom he had noted, as he passed the first time, took away all hope that it might be supposed the act of a momentary madness without premeditation. The doctor had told his story with all the precision that was natural to him before he knew who it was that would be convicted by it; and now it was no longer possible for him, even had his conscience permitted it, to soften the details which he had at first given so clearly, or to throw any mist upon his clear narrative. He had to repeat it all, knowing the fatal effect it must have, standing up with Jim's pale face before him, with a knowledge that somewhere in a dim corner Agnes sat with bowed head listening—to what she already knew so well. The doctor's countenance was as pale as Jim's. His mouth grew dry as he bore his testimony; but not all the terrible consequences could make him alter a word. He could scarcely refrain a groan, a sob, when he had done; and this involuntary evidence of what it cost him to tell the truth increased the effect in the highest degree, as the evidence of an unwilling witness always does. There was but one point in which he could help the prisoner; and fortunately that too had been a special point in his previous evidence: but it was not until Dr. Barrère got into the hands of Jim's advocate that this was brought out. "I see," the counsel said, "that in your previous examination you speak of a cry uttered by the assailant after the blows which you have described. You describe it as a cry of horror. In what sense do you mean this to be understood?"

"I mean," said Dr. Barrère very pointedly and clearly—and if there had been any divided attention in the crowded court where so many people had come to hear the fate of one whom they had known from his childhood, every mind was roused now, and every eye intent upon the speaker—"I mean—" He paused to give fuller force to what he said.

"I mean that the man who struck those blows for the first time realised what he was doing. The cry was one of consternation and dismay. It was the cry of a man horrified to see what he had done."

"The cry was so remarkable that it made a great impression on your mind?"

"A very great impression. I do not think I have ever heard an utterance which affected me so much."

"You were hurrying forward at the time to interpose in the scuffle. Did you distinguish any words? Did you recognise the voice?"

"It would give an erroneous impression to say that I meant to interpose in the scuffle. There was no scuffle. The man fell at once. He never had a chance of defending himself. I did not recognise the voice, nor can I say that any words were used. It was nothing but a cry."

"The cry, however, was of such a nature as to induce you to change your mind in respect to what had occurred?"

"I had no time to form any theory. The impression it produced on my mind was that an assault was intended, but not murder; and that all at once it had become apparent to the unfortunate—" Here the doctor paused, and there was a deep sobbing breath of intense attention drawn by the crowd. He stopped for a minute, and then resumed, "It had become apparent to the—assailant that he had—gone too far; that the consequences were more terrible than he had intended. He threw down what he had in his hand, and fled in horror."

"You were convinced, then, that there was no murderous intention in the act of the unfortunate—as you have well said—assailant?"

"That was my conviction," said Dr. Barrère.

The effect made upon the assembly was great. And though it was no doubt diminished more or less by the cross-examination of the counsel for the prosecution, who protested vehemently against the epithet of unfortunate applied to the man who had attacked in the dark another man who was proceeding quietly about his own business, who had lain in wait for him and assaulted him murderously with every evidence of premeditation, it still remained the strongest point in the defence. "You say that you had no time to form any theory?" said the prosecutor; "yet you have told us that you rushed forward calling out murder. Was this before or after you heard the cry, so full of meaning, which you have described?"

"It was probably almost at the same moment," said Dr. Barrère.

"Yet, even in the act of crying out murder, you were capable of noticing all the complicated sentiments which you now tell us were in the assailant's cry!"

"In great excitement one takes no notice of the passage of time—a minute contains as much as an hour."

"And you expect us to believe that in that minute, and without the help of words, you were enlightened as to the meaning of the act by a mere inarticulate cry?"

"I tell you the impression produced on my mind, as I told it at the coroner's inquest," said Dr. Barrère, steadily; "as I have told it to my friends from the first."

"Yet this did not prevent you from shouting murder?"

"No; it did not prevent me from calling for help in the usual way."

This was all that could be made of the doctor. It remained the strongest point in poor Jim's favour, who was, as everybody saw to be inevitable, condemned; yet recommended to mercy because of what Dr. Barrère had said. Otherwise there were many features in the case that roused the popular pity. The bad character of the man who had been killed, the evil influence he was known to have exercised, the injury he had done to Jim himself and to so many others, and the very cause of the quarrel in which Jim had threatened and announced his intention of punishing him—all these things, had Jim been tried in France, would have produced a verdict modified by extenuating circumstances. In England it did not touch the decision, but it produced that vague recommendation to mercy with which pity satisfies itself when it can do no more.

Dr. Barrère took the unfortunate mother and sister home. Mrs. Surtees, broken as she was, could not be absent from the court when her son's fate was to be determined. She was as one stricken dumb as they took her back. Now and then she would put her trembling hands to her eyes as if expecting tears which did not come. Her very heart and soul were crushed by the awful doom which had been spoken. And the others did not even dare to exchange a look. The horror which enveloped them was too terrible for speech. It was only after an interval had passed, and life, indomitable life which always rises again whatever may be the anguish that subdues it for a moment, had returned in pain and fear to its struggle with the intolerable, that words and the power of communication returned. Then Dr. Barrère told the broken-hearted women that both he himself and others in the town who knew Jim, with all the influence that could be brought to bear, would work for a revision of the sentence. It was upon his own evidence that the hopes which those who were not so deeply, tremendously interested, but who regarded the case with an impartial eye, began to entertain, were founded. "I hope that the Home Secretary may send for me," he said; "they think he will. God grant it!" He too had worked himself into a kind of hope.

"Oh," said Agnes, melting for the first time into tears at the touch of a possible deliverance, "if we could go, as they used to do, to the Queen, his mother and his sister, on our knees!"

Mrs. Surtees sat and listened to them with her immovable face of misery. "Don't speak to me of hope, for I cannot bear it," she said. "Oh, don't speak of hope; there is none—none! Nothing but death and shame."

"Yes, mother," said Dr. Barrère, and he added under his breath, "whatever happens—whatever happens—there shall be no death of shame."

CHAPTER V

The recommendation to mercy was very strong; almost all the principal people in the town interested themselves, and the judge himself had been persuaded to add a potent word; but as he did so he shook his head, and told the petitioners that their arguments were all sentimental. "What does your lordship say then to the doctor's testimony?" was asked him, upon which he shook his head more and more. "The doctor's testimony, above all," he said. "Mind you, I think that probably the doctor was right, but it is not a solid argument, it is all sentiment; and that is what the Home Office makes no account of." This was very discouraging. But still there was a certain enthusiasm in the town in Jim's favour, as well as a natural horror that one who really belonged (if he had kept his position) to the best class, should come to such an end; and the chief people who got up this recommendation to mercy were warm supporters of the Government. That, too, they felt convinced must tell for something. And there reigned in Poolborough a certain hope which Dr. Barrère sometimes shared.

Sometimes; for on many occasions he took the darker view—the view so universal and generally received, that the more important it is for you that a certain thing should come to pass, the more you desire it, the less likely it is to happen. And then he would ask himself was it so important that it should come to pass? At the best it was still true that Jim had killed this man. If he were not hanged for it he would be imprisoned for life; and whether it is worse to have a relative who has been hanged for a crime or one who is lingering out a long term of imprisonment for it, it is hard to tell. There did not seem much to choose between them. Perhaps even the hanging would be forgotten soonest—and it would be less of a burden. For to think of a brother in prison, who might emerge years hence with a ticket-of-leave, a disgraced and degraded man, was something terrible. Perhaps on the whole it would be best that he should die. And then Dr. Barrère shuddered. Die! Ah! if that might be, quietly, without demonstration. But as it was—And then he would begin again, against his will, that painful circle of thought—"the brother was hanged." That was what people would say. After the horror of it had died out fantastic patients would cry, "The brother of a man who was hanged! Oh, no! don't let us call in such a person." The ladies would say this: they would shudder yet perhaps even laugh, for the pity would be forgotten, even the horror would be forgotten, and there would remain only this suggestion of discomfort—just enough to make the women feel that they would not like to have him, the brother of a man who was hanged, for their doctor. Dr. Barrère tried all he could to escape from this circle of fatal thought; but however hard he worked, and however much he occupied himself, he could not do so always. And the thought went near sometimes to make him mad.

He had, however, much to occupy him, to keep thought away. He was the only element of comfort in the life of the two miserable women who lived under the shadow of death, their minds entirely absorbed in the approaching catastrophe, living through it a hundred times in anticipation, in despair which was made more ghastly and sickening by a flicker of terrible hope. Mrs. Surtees said that she had no hope; she would not allow the possibility to be named; but secretly dwelt upon it with an intensity of suspense which was more unendurable than any calamity. And when Agnes and her lover were alone this was the subject that occupied them to the exclusion of all others. Their own hopes and prospects were all blotted out as if they had never been. He brought her reports of what was said, and what was thought on the subject among the people who had influence, those who were straining every nerve to obtain a reprieve: and she hung upon his words breathless with an all-absorbing interest. He never got beyond the awful shadow, or could forget it, and went about all day with that cloud hanging over him, and frightened his patients with his stern and serious looks. "Dr. Barrère is not an encouraging doctor," they began to say, "he makes you think you are going to die;" for the sick people could not divest themselves of the idea that it was their complaints that were foremost in the doctor's mind and produced that severity in his looks.

But all this was light and easy to the last of the many occupations which filled Dr. Barrère's time and thoughts, and that was Jim—Jim alone in his prison, he who never had been alone, who had been surrounded all day long with his companions—the companions who had led him astray. No, they had not led him astray. Langton, who was dead, whom he had killed, had not led him astray, though he now thought so, or said so, bemoaning himself. Such a thing would be too heavy a burden for any human spirit. A man cannot ruin any more than he can save his brother. His own inclinations, his own will, his love for the forbidden, his idle wishes and follies—these were what had led him astray. And now he was left alone to think of all that, with the shadow before him of a hideous death at a fixed moment—a moment drawing nearer and nearer, which he could no more escape than he could forget it. Jim had many good qualities amid his evil ones. He was not a bad man; his sins were rather those of a foolish, self-indulgent boy. His character was that of a boy. A certain innocency, if that word may be used, lay under the surface of his vices, and long confinement away from all temptation had wrought a change in him like that that came over the leper in the Scriptures, whose flesh came again as the flesh of a little child. This was what happened to Jim, both bodily and mentally. He languished in health from his confinement, but yet his eyes regained the clearness of his youth, and his mind, all its ingenuousness, its power of affection. Lying under sentence of death he became once more the lovable human creature, the winning and attractive youth he had been in the days before trouble came. All clouds save the one cloud rolled off his soul. In all likelihood he himself forgot the course of degradation through which he had gone; everything was obliterated to him by the impossibility of sinning more—everything except the one thing which no self-delusion could obliterate, the unchangeable doom to which he was approaching day by day. Jim had none of the tremors of a murderer. He concealed nothing; he admitted freely that the verdict was just, that it was he who had lurked in the dark and awaited the villain—but only he had never meant more than to punish him. "It is all quite true what the doctor says. I knocked him down. I meant to beat him within an inch of his life. God knows if he deserved it at my hands, or any honest man's hands. And then it came over me in a moment that he never moved, that he never made a struggle. It was not because there were people coming up that I ran away. It was horror, as the doctor says. Nothing can ever happen to me again so dreadful as that," said Jim, putting up his handkerchief to wipe his damp forehead. And yet he could tell even that story with tolerable calm. He was not conscious of guilt; he had meant to do what he felt quite justifiable—rather laudable than otherwise—to thrash a rascal "within an inch of his life." He had expected the man to defend himself; he had been full of what he felt to be righteous rage, and he did not feel himself guilty now. He was haunted by no ghost; he had ceased even to shudder at the recollection of the horrible moment in which he became aware that instead of chastising he had killed. But when his momentary occupation with other thoughts died away and the recollection of what lay before him came back, the condition of poor Jim was a dreadful one. To die—for that!—to die on Thursday, the 3rd of September, at a horrible moment fixed and unchangeable. To feel the days running past remorselessly, swift, without an event to break their monotonous flying pace—those days which were so endlessly long from dawn to twilight, which seemed as if they would never be done, which had so little night, yet which flew noiselessly, silently, bringing him ever nearer and nearer to the end. Poor Jim broke down entirely under the pressure of this intolerable certainty. Had it been done at once, the moment the sentence had been pronounced; but to sit and wait for it, look for it, anticipate it, know that every hour was bringing it nearer, that through the dark and through the day, and through all the endless circles of thoughts that surmounted and surrounded it, it was coming, always coming, not to be escaped! Jim's nerves broke down under this intolerable thing that had to be borne. He kept command of himself when he saw his mother and sister, but with Dr. Barrère he let himself go. It was a relief to him for the wretched moment. Save for the moment, nothing, alas, could be a relief—for whether he contrived to smile and subdue himself, or whether he dashed himself against the wall of impossibility that shut him in, whether he raved in anguish or madness, or slept, or tried to put a brave face upon it, it was coming all the time.

"It is sitting and waiting that is the horrible thing," he said; "to think there is nothing you can do. That's true, you know, doctor, in Don Juan, about the people that plunged into the sea to get drowned a little sooner and be done with it—in the shipwreck, you know. It's waiting and seeing it coming that is horrible. It is just thirteen days to-day. Death isn't what I mind! it's waiting for it. Will it be—will it be very—horrible, do you think—at the moment—when it comes?"

"No," said Dr. Barrère, "if it comes to that, not horrible at all—a moment, no more."

"A moment—but you can't tell till you try what may be in a moment. I don't mind, doctor; something sharp and soon would be a sort of relief. It is the sitting and waiting, counting the days, seeing it coming—always coming. Nobody has a right to torture a fellow like that—let them take him and hang him as the lynchers do, straight off." Then Jim was seized with a slight convulsive shudder. "And then the afterwards, doctor? for all your science you can't tell anything about that. Perhaps you don't believe in it at all. I do."

Dr. Barrère made no reply. He was not quite clear about what he believed; and he had nothing to say on such a subject to this young man standing upon the verge, with all the uncertainties and possibilities of life still so warm in him, and yet so near the one unalterable certainty. After a minute Jim resumed.

"I do," he said firmly. "I've never been what you call a skeptic. I don't believe men are: they only pretend, or perhaps think so, till it comes upon them. I wonder what they'll say to a poor fellow up there, doctor? I've always been told they understand up there—there can't be injustice done like here. And I've always been a true believer. I've never been led away—like that."

"It isn't a subject on which I can talk," said the doctor, unsteadily; "your mother and Agnes, they know. But, Jim, for the love of God don't talk to them as you are doing now. Put on a good face for their sakes."

"Poor mother!" said Jim. He turned all at once almost to crying—softened entirely out of his wild talk. "What has she done to have a thing like this happen to her? She is a real good woman—and to have a son hanged, good Lord!" Again he shivered convulsively. "She won't live long, that's one thing; and perhaps it'll be explained to her satisfaction up there. But that's what I call unjust, Barrère, to torture a poor soul like that, that has never done anything but good all her life. You'll take care of Agnes. But mother will not live long, poor dear. Poor dear!" he repeated with a tremulous smile. "I suppose she had a happy life till I grew up—till I—I wonder what I could be born for, a fellow like me, to be hanged!" he cried with a sudden, sharp anguish in which there was the laughter of misery and the groan of despair.

Dr. Barrère left the prison with his heart bleeding; but he did not abandon Jim. On the contrary, there was a terrible attraction which drew him to the presence of the unfortunate young man. The doctor of Poolborough jail, though not so high in the profession as himself, was one of Dr. Barrère's acquaintances, and to him he went when he left the condemned cell. The doctor told his professional brother that Surtees was in a very bad state of health. "His nerves have broken down entirely. His heart—haven't you remarked?—his heart is in such a state that he might go at any moment."

"Dear me," said the other, "he has never complained that I know of. And a very good thing, too, Barrère; you don't mean to say that you would regret it if anything did happen, before—"

"No," said the doctor, "but the poor fellow may suffer. I wonder if you'd let me have the charge of him, Maxwell? I know you're a busy man. And it would please his mother to think that I was looking after him. What do you say?"

The one medical man looked at the other. Doctor Barrère was pale, but he did not shrink from the look turned upon him. "I'll tell you what I'll do, Barrère," said the prison doctor at last. "I'm getting all wrong for want of a little rest. Feel my hand—my nerves are as much shaken as Surtees'! If you'll take the whole for a fortnight, so that I may take my holiday—"

Dr. Barrère thought for a moment. "A fortnight? That will be till after—I don't know how I'm to do it with my practice; but I will do it, for the sake of—your health, Maxwell: for I see you are in a bad way."

"Hurrah!" said the other, "a breath of air will set me all right, and I shall be forever obliged to you, Barrère." Then he stopped for a moment and looked keenly in his face. "You're a better man than I am, and know more: but for God's sake, Barrère, no tricks—no tricks. You know what I mean," he said.

"No, I don't know what you mean. I know you want a holiday, and I want to take care of a case in which I am interested. It suits us both. Let me have all the details you can," said Dr. Barrère.

CHAPTER VI

The day had come, and almost the hour. The weary time had stolen, endless, yet flying on noiseless wings; an eternity of featureless lingering hours, yet speeding, speeding towards that one fixed end. And there was no reprieve. The important people of Poolborough had retired sullenly from their endeavours. To support a Government faithfully and yet not to have one poor favour granted—their recommendation to mercy turned back upon themselves; they were indignant, and in that grievance they forgot the original cause of it. Still there were one or two still toiling on. But the morning of the fatal day had dawned and nothing had come.

To tell how Mrs. Surtees and Agnes had lived through these days is beyond our power. They did not live; they dragged through a feverish dream from one time of seeing him to another, unconscious what passed in the meantime, except when some messenger would come to their door, and a wild blaze and frenzy of hope would light up in their miserable hearts: for it always seemed to them that it must be the reprieve which was coming, though each said to herself that it would not, could not, come. And when they saw Jim, that one actual recurring point in their lives was perhaps more miserable than the intervals. For to see him, and to know that the hour was coming ever nearer and nearer when he must die; to sit with him, never free from inspection, never out of hearing of some compulsory spectator; to see the tension of his nerves, the strain of intolerable expectation in him—was almost more than flesh and blood could bear. They had privileges which were not allowed in ordinary cases—for were not they still ranked among the best people of Poolborough, though beaten down by horrible calamity? What could they say to him? Not even the religious exhortations, the prayers which came from other lips less trembling. They were dumb. "Dear Jim," and "God bless you," was all they could say. Their misery was too great, there was no utterance in it; a word would have overthrown the enforced and awful calm. And neither could he speak. When he had said "Mother," and kissed her, and smiled, that was all. Then they sat silent holding each other's hands.

Through all this Dr. Barrère was the only human supporter of the miserable family. He had promised to stand by Jim, to the end, not to leave him till life had left him—till all was over. And now the supreme moment had nearly come. The doctor was as pale, almost paler than he who was about to die. There was an air about him of sternness, almost of desperation; yet to Jim he was tender as his mother. He had warned the authorities what he feared, that agitation and excitement might even yet rob the law of its victim. He had been allowed to be with the condemned man from earliest dawn of the fatal morning in consequence of the warning he had given, but it appeared to the attendants that Jim himself bore a less alarming air than the doctor, whose colourless face and haggard eyes looked as if he had not slept for a week. Jim, poor Jim, had summoned all his courage for this supreme moment. There was a sweetness in his look that added to its youthfulness. He looked like a boy: his long imprisonment and the enforced self-denial there was in it, had chased from his face all stains of evil. He was pale and worn with his confinement and with the interval of awful waiting, but his eyes were clear as a child's—pathetic, tender, with a wistful smile in them, as though the arrival of the fatal hour had brought relief. The old clergyman who had baptised him had come, too, to stand by him to the last, and he could scarcely speak for tears. But Jim was calm, and smiled; if any bit of blue sky was in that cell of the condemned, with all its grim and melancholy memories, it was in Jim's face.

The doctor moved about him not able to keep still, with that look of desperation, listening for every sound. But all was still except the broken voice of the old clergyman, who had knelt down and was praying. One of the attendants too had gone down on his knees. The other stood watching, yet distracted by a pity which even his hardened faculties could not resist. Jim sat with his hands clasped, his eyes for a moment closed, the smile still quivering about his mouth. In this stillness of intense feeling all observation save that of the ever-watchful doctor was momentarily subdued. Suddenly Jim's head seemed to droop forward on his breast; the doctor came in front of him with one swift step, and through the sound of the praying called imperatively, sharply, for wine, wine! The warder who was standing rushed to fill it out, while Dr. Barrère bent over the fainting youth. It all passed in a moment, before the half-said sentence of the prayer was completed. The clergyman's voice wavered, stopped—and then resumed again, finishing the phrase, notwithstanding the stir and hurried movement, the momentary breathless scuffle, which a sudden attack of illness, a fit or faint, always occasions. Then a sharp sound broke the stillness—the crash of the wine glass which the doctor let fall from his hand after forcing the contents, as it seemed, down the patient's throat. The old clergyman on his knees still, paused and opening his eyes gazed at the strange scene, not awakening to the seriousness of it, or perceiving any new element introduced into the solemnity of the situation for some minutes, yet gazing with tragic eyes, since nothing in the first place could well be more tragic. The little stir, the scuffle of the moving feet, the two men in motion about the still figure in the chair, lasted for a little longer; then the warder uttered a stifled cry. The clergyman on his knees, his heart still in his prayer for the dying, felt it half profane to break off into words to men in the midst of those he was addressing to God—but forced by this strange break cried, "What is it?—what has happened?" in spite of himself.

There was no immediate answer. The doctor gave some brief, quick directions, and with the help of the warder lifted the helpless figure, all fallen upon itself like a ruined house, with difficulty to the bed. The limp, long, helpless limbs, the entire immobility and deadness of the form struck with a strange chill to the heart of the man who had been interceding wrapt in another atmosphere than that of earth. The clergyman got up from his knees, coming back with a keen and awful sense of his humanity. "Has he—fainted?" he asked with a gasp.

Once more a dead pause, a stillness in which the four men heard their hearts beating; then the doctor said, with a strange brevity and solemnity, "Better than that—he is dead."

Dead! They gathered round and gazed in a consternation beyond words. The young face, scarcely paler than it had been a moment since, the eyes half shut, the lips fallen apart with that awful opening which is made by the exit of the last breath, lay back upon the wretched pillow in all that abstraction and incalculable distance which comes with the first touch of death. No one could look at that, and be in any doubt. The warders stood by dazed with horror and dismay, as if they had let their prisoner escape. Was it their fault? Would they be blamed for it? They had seen men go to the scaffold before with little feeling, but they had never seen one die of the horror of it, as Jim had died.

While they were thus standing a sound of measured steps was heard without. The door was opened with that harsh turning of the key which in other circumstances would have sounded like the trumpet of doom, but which now woke no tremor, scarcely any concern. It was the sheriff and his grim procession coming for the prisoner. They streamed in and gathered astonished about the bed. Dr. Barrère turned from where he stood at the head, with a face which was like ashes—pallid, stern, the nostrils dilating, the throat held high. He made a solemn gesture with his hand towards the bed. "You come too late," he said.

The men had come in almost silently, in the excitement of the moment swelling the sombre circle to a little crowd. They thronged upon each other and looked at him, lying there on the miserable prison bed, in the light of the horrible grated windows, all awe-stricken in a kind of grey consternation not knowing how to believe it; for it was a thing unparalleled that one who was condemned should thus give his executioner the slip. The whisper of the sheriff's low voice inquiring into the catastrophe broke the impression a little. "How did it happen—how was it? Dead! But it seems impossible. Are you sure, doctor, it is not a faint?"

The doctor waved his hand almost scornfully towards the still and rigid form. "I foresaw it always; it is—as I thought it would be," he said.

"His poor mother!" said the clergyman with a sort of habitual, conventional lamentation, as if it could matter to that poor mother! Dr. Barrère turned upon him quickly. "Go to them—tell them—it will save them something," he said with sudden eagerness. "You can do no more here."

"It seems impossible," the sheriff repeated, turning again to the bed. "Is there a glass to be had?—anything—hold it to his lips! Do something, doctor. Have you tried all means? are you sure?" He had no doubt; but astonishment, and the novelty of the situation, suggested questions which really required no answer. He touched the dead hand and shuddered. "It is extraordinary, most extraordinary," he said.

"I warned you of the possibility from the beginning," said Dr. Barrère; "his heart was very weak. It is astonishing rather that he bore the strain so long." Then he added with that stern look, "It is better that it should be so."

The words were scarcely out of his lips when a sudden commotion was heard as of some one hurrying along the stony passages, a sound of voices and hasty steps. The door which, in view of the fatal ceremonial about to take place, had been left open, was pushed quickly, loudly to the wall, and an important personage, the Mayor of Poolborough, flushed and full of excitement, hurried in. "Thank God," he cried, wiping his forehead, "thank God, it's come in time! I knew they could not refuse us. Here is the reprieve come at last."

A cry, a murmur rose into the air from all the watchers. Who could help it? The reprieve—at such a moment! This solemn mockery was more than human nerves could bear. The warder who had been poor Jim's chief guardian broke forth into a sudden loud outburst, like a child's, of crying. The sheriff could not speak. He pointed silently to the bed.

But of all the bystanders none was moved like Dr. Barrère. He fell backward as if he had received a blow, and gazed at the mayor speechless, his under lip dropping, his face livid, heavy drops coming out upon his brow. It was not till he was appealed to in the sudden explanations that followed that the doctor came to himself. When he was addressed he seemed to wake as from a dream, and answered with difficulty; his lips parched, his throat dry, making convulsive efforts to moisten his tongue, and enunciate the necessary words. "Heart disease—feared all the time—" he said, as if he had partly lost that faculty of speech. The mayor looked sharply at him, as if suspecting something. What was it? intoxication? So early, and at such a time? But Dr. Barrère seemed to have lost all interest in what was proceeding. He cared nothing for their looks. He cared for nothing in the world. "I'm of no further use here," he said huskily, and went toward the door as if he were blind, pushing against one and another. When he had reached the door, however, he turned back. "The poor fellow," he said, "the poor—victim was to be given to his family after—. It was a favour granted them. The removal was to be seen to—to-night; there is no reason for departing from that arrangement, I suppose?"

The officials looked at each other, not knowing what to say, feeling that in the unexpected catastrophe there was something which demanded a change, yet unable on the spur of the moment to think what it was. Then the mayor replied faltering, "I suppose so. It need not make any change, do you think? The poor family—have enough to bear without, vexing them with alterations. Since there can be—no doubt—" He paused and looked, and shuddered. No doubt, oh, no doubt! The execution would have been conducted with far less sensation. It was strange that such a shivering of horror should overwhelm them to see him lying so still upon that bed.

"Now I must go—to my rounds," the doctor said. He went out, buttoning up his coat to his throat, as if he were shivering too, though it was a genial September morning, soft and warm. He went out from the dark prison walls into the sunshine like a man dazed, passing the horrible preparations on his way, the coffin! from which he shrank as if it had been a monster. Dr. Barrère's countenance was like that of a dead man. He walked straight before him as if he were going somewhere; but he went upon no rounds; his patients waited for him vainly. He walked and walked till fatigue of the body produced a general stupor, aiding and completing the strange collapse of the mind, and then mechanically, but not till it was evening, he went home. His housekeeper, full of anxious questions, was silenced by the look of his face, and had his dinner placed hastily and silently upon the table, thinking the agitation of the day had been too much for him. Dr. Barrère neither ate nor drank, but he fell into a heavy and troubled sleep at the table, where he had seated himself mechanically. It was late when he woke, and dark, and for a moment there was a pause of bewilderment and confusion in his mind. Then he rose, went to his desk and took some money out of it, and his cheque-book. He took up an overcoat as he went through the hall. He did not so much as hear the servant's timid question as to when he should return. When he should return!

After the body of poor Jim had been brought back to his mother's house and all was silent there, in that profound hush after an expected calamity which is almost a relief, Agnes, not able to rest, wondering in her misery why all that day her lover had not come near them, had not sent any communication, but for the first time had abandoned them in their sorrow, stood for a moment by the window in the hall to look if, by any possibility, he might still be coming. He might have been detained by some pressing call. He had neglected everything for Jim; he might now be compelled to make up for it—who could tell? Some reason there must be for his desertion. As she went to the window, which was on a level with the street, it gave her a shock beyond expression to see a pallid face close to it looking in—a miserable face, haggard, with eyes that were bloodshot and red, while everything else was the colour of clay—the colour of death. It was with difficulty she restrained a scream. She opened the window softly and said:

"Arnold! you have come at last!" The figure outside shrank and withdrew, then said, "Do not touch me—don't look at me. I did it: to save him the shame—"

"Arnold, come in, for God's sake! Don't speak so—Arnold—"

"Never, never more! I thought the reprieve would not come. I did it. Oh, never, never more!"

"Arnold!" she cried, stretching out her hands. But he was gone. Opening the door as quickly as her trembling would let her, the poor girl looked out into the dark street, into the night: but there was no one there.

Was it a dream, a vision, an illusion of exhausted nature, unable to discern reality from imagination? No one ever knew; but from that night Dr. Barrère was never seen more in Poolborough, nor did any of those who had known him hear of him again. He disappeared as if he had never been. And if that was the terrible explanation of it, or if the sudden shock had maddened him, or if it was really he that Agnes saw, no one can tell. But it was the last that was ever heard or seen of Dr. Barrère.

Margaret Oliphant – A Short Biography

Margaret Oliphant Wilson was born on April 4th, 1828 to Francis W. Wilson, a clerk, and Margaret Oliphant, at Wallyford, near Musselburgh, East Lothian.

She spent her childhood at Lasswade, near Dalkeith, Glasgow before moving to Liverpool.

Her youth was spent in establishing a writing style so much so that, in 1849, she had her first novel published: Passages in the Life of Mrs. Margaret Maitland based on the Scottish Free Church movement. It met with some success and was a good start to her career.

Two years later, in 1851, her third book Caleb Field was published. It was also now that she met the publisher William Blackwood in Edinburgh and was asked to contribute to his well-received Blackwood's Magazine. It was to be a lifelong endeavor. Over the course of the relationship she would have well over 100 articles published.

In May 1852, Margaret married her cousin, Frank Wilson Oliphant, at Birkenhead, and they settled at Harrington Square, Camden, London. He was an artist working primarily in stained glass. With the marriage she became Margaret Oliphant Wilson Oliphant.

Their marriage produced six children but three tragically died in infancy.

When her husband developed signs of the dreaded consumption (tuberculosis) they moved, on the advice of doctors, to warmer climes. In January 1859 it was to Florence, and then to Rome where, sadly, he died.

Margaret was naturally devastated but was also now left without support and only her income from her writing. She returned to England and took up the task of supporting her three remaining children by her literary activity.

By now she was being published both as an established novelist and regularly in Blackwood's Magazine, amongst several others. Her incredible and prolific work rate increased both her commercial reputation and the size of her reading audience.

Against this her domestic life continued to be tragic, full of sorrow and disappointment.

In January 1864 her only remaining daughter, Maggie, died and was buried in her father's grave in Rome. Her brother, who had emigrated to Canada, was shortly afterwards involved in financial ruin. Margaret generously offered a home to him and his children, adding another demand to her already heavy responsibilities.

In 1866 she settled at Windsor to be closer to her sons, who were being educated at near-by Eton School. That year, her second cousin, Annie Louisa Walker, came to live with her as a companion-housekeeper. Windsor was now to be her home for the rest of her life.

Her literary career for three decades was one of constant delivery and success. Whether she wrote historical works or across several genres in fiction: domestic realism, historical, romance or supernatural she was successful.

For more than thirty years she pursued a varied literary career but family life continued to bring problems.

The literary ambitions she wished for her sons were unfulfilled. Cyril Francis, the eldest, died in 1890, leaving a Life of Alfred de Musset, which was later incorporated in his mother's Foreign Classics for English Readers. The younger, Francis, who she nicknamed 'Cecco', collaborated with her in the Victorian Age of English Literature and won a position at the British Museum, but was rejected by Sir Andrew Clark, a famous physician. Cecco died in 1894.

With the last of her children now lost to her, she had but little further interest in life. Her health steadily and inexorably declined.

Margaret Oliphant Wilson Oliphant died at the age of 69 in Wimbledon on 20th June 1897. She is buried in Eton beside her sons.

At her death, Margaret was still working on Annals of a Publishing House, a record of Blackwood's Magazine with which she had enjoyed such a successful relationship.

Her Autobiography and Letters, which present a thoughtful picture of her domestic anxieties, was published in 1899. Only parts were written with a wider audience in mind: she had originally intended the Autobiography for her son, but he died before she could finish it.

Opinions on Oliphant's work are split, with some critics seeing her as a 'domestic novelist', while others recognize her work as influential and important to the Victorian literature canon. Critical reception from her contemporaries is also divided. John Skelton took the view that Oliphant wrote too much and too quickly. Writing a Blackwood's article called 'A Little Chat About Mrs. Oliphant', he asked, "Had Mrs. Oliphant concentrated her powers, what might she not have done? We might have had another Charlotte Brontë or another George Eliot." However not all of the contemporary reception was negative. The esteemed M. R. James admired Oliphant's supernatural fiction, concluding that "the religious ghost story, as it may be called, was never done better than by Mrs. Oliphant in 'The Open Door' and 'A Beleaguered City'. Mary Butts lavished praise on Oliphant's ghost story 'The Library Window', describing it as "one masterpiece of sober loveliness".

More modern critics of Oliphant's work include Virginia Woolf, who asked in 'Three Guineas' whether Oliphant's autobiography does not lead the reader "to deplore the fact that Mrs. Oliphant sold her brain, her very admirable brain, prostituted her culture and enslaved her intellectual liberty in order that she might earn her living and educate her children."

Whatever the merits of their cases Margaret Oliphant has been shamefully neglected in modern years. She is now becoming more widely recognised as a leading writer of her day.

Margaret Oliphant – A Concise Bibliography

A canon of more than 120 works, including novels, travel books, histories, and volumes of literary criticism.

Novels
Margaret Maitland (1849)
Merkland (1850)
Caleb Field (1851)
John Drayton (1851)
Adam Graeme (1852)
The Melvilles (1852)
Katie Stewart (1852)
Harry Muir (1853)

Ailieford (1853)
The Quiet Heart (1854)
Magdalen Hepburn (1854)
Zaidee (1855)
Lilliesleaf (1855)
Christian Melville (1855)
The Athelings (1857)
The Days of My Life (1857)
Orphans (1858)
The Laird of Norlaw (1858)
Agnes Hopetoun's Schools and Holidays (1859)
Lucy Crofton (1860)
The House on the Moor (1861)
The Last of the Mortimers (1862)
Heart and Cross (1863)
Salem Chapel (1863)
The Rector (1863)
Doctor's Family (1863)
The Perpetual Curate (1864)
Miss Marjoribanks (1866)
Phoebe Junior (1876)
A Son of the Soil (1865)
Agnes (1866)
Madonna Mary (1867)
Brownlows (1868)
The Minister's Wife (1869)
The Three Brothers (1870)
John: A Love Story (1870)
Squire Arden (1871)
At his Gates (1872)
Ombra (1872
May (1873)
Innocent (1873)
The Story of Valentine and His Brother (1875)
A Rose in June (1874)
For Love and Life (1874)
Whiteladies (1875)
An Odd Couple (1875)
The Curate in Charge (1876)
Carità (1877)
Young Musgrave (1877)
Mrs. Arthur (1877)
The Primrose Path (1878)
Within the Precincts (1879)
The Fugitives (1879)
A Beleaguered City (1879)
The Greatest Heiress in England (1880)
He That Will Not When He May (1880)

In Trust (1881)
Harry Joscelyn (1881)
Lady Jane (1882)
A Little Pilgrim in the Unseen (1882)
The Lady Lindores (1883)
Sir Tom (1883)
Hester (1883)
It Was a Lover and his Lass (1883)
The Lady's Walk (1883)
The Wizard's Son (1884)
Madam (1884)
The Prodigals and Their Inheritance (1885)
Oliver's Bride (1885)
A Country Gentleman and His Family (1886)
A House Divided Against Itself (1886)
Effie Ogilvie (1886)
A Poor Gentleman (1886)
The Son of His Father (1886)
Joyce (1888)
Cousin Mary (1888)
The Land of Darkness (1888)
Lady Car (1889)
Kirsteen (1890)
The Mystery of Mrs. Biencarrow (1890)
Sons and Daughters (1890)
The Railway Man and His Children (1891)
The Heir Presumptive and the Heir Apparent (1891)
The Marriage of Elinor (1891)
Janet (1891)
The Cuckoo in the Nest (1892)
Diana Trelawny (1892)
The Sorceress (1893)
A House in Bloomsbury (1894)
Sir Robert's Fortune (1894)
Who Was Lost and is Found (1894)
Lady William (1894)
Two Strangers (1895)
Old Mr. Tredgold (1895)
The Unjust Steward (1896)
The Ways of Life (1897)

Short stories
Neighbours on the Green (1889)
A Widow's Tale and Other Stories (1898)
That Little Cutty (1898)
The Open Door (1918)

Selected Articles
Mary Russel Mitford (Blackwood's Magazine, Vol. 75, 1854)
Evelin and Pepys (Blackwood's Magazine, Vol. 76, 1854)
The Holy Land (Blackwood's Magazine, Vol. 76, 1854)
Mr. Thackeray and his Novels (Blackwood's Magazine, Vol. 77, 1855)
Bulwer (Blackwood's Magazine, Vol. 77, 1855)
Charles Dickens (Blackwood's Magazine, Vol. 77, 1855)
Modern Novelists—Great and Small (Blackwood's Magazine, Vol. 77, 1855)
Modern Light Literature: Poetry (Blackwood's Magazine, Vol. 79, 1856)
Religion in Common Life (Blackwood's Magazine, Vol. 79, 1856)
Sydney Smith (Blackwood's Magazine, Vol. 79, 1856)
The Laws Concerning Women (Blackwood's Magazine, Vol. 79, 1856)
The Art of Caviling (Blackwood's Magazine, Vol. 80, 1856)
Béranger (Blackwood's Magazine, Vol. 83, 1858)
The Condition of Women (Blackwood's Magazine, Vol. 83, 1858)
The Missionary Explorer (Blackwood's Magazine, Vol. 83, 1858)
Religious Memoirs (Blackwood's Magazine, Vol. 83, 1858)
Social Science (Blackwood's Magazine, Vol. 88, 1860)
Scotland and her Accusers (Blackwood's Magazine, Vol. 90, 1861)
The Chronicles of Carlingford (Blackwood's Magazine 1862–1865)
Girolamo Savonarola (Blackwood's Magazine, Vol. 93, 1863)
The Life of Jesus (Blackwood's Magazine, Vol. 96, 1864)
Giacomo Leopardi (Blackwood's Magazine, Vol. 98, 1865)
The Great Unrepresented (Blackwood's Magazine, Vol. 100, 1866)
Mill on the Subjection of Women (The Edinburgh Review, Vol. 130, 1869)
The Opium-Eater (Blackwood's Magazine, Vol. 122, 1877)
Russian and Nihilism in the Novels of I. Tourgeniéf (Blackwood's Magazine, Vol. 127, 1880)
School and College (Blackwood's Magazine, Vol. 128, 1880)
The Grievances of Women (Fraser's Magazine, New Series, Vol. 21, 1880)
Mrs. Carlyle (The Contemporary Review, Vol. 43, May 1883)
The Ethics of Biography (The Contemporary Review, July 1883)
Victor Hugo (The Contemporary Review, Vol. 48, July/December 1885)
A Venetian Dynasty (The Contemporary Review, Vol. 50, August 1886)
Laurence Oliphant (Blackwood's Magazine, Vol. 145, 1889)
Tennyson (Blackwood's Magazine, Vol. 152, 1892)
Addison, the Humorist (Century Magazine, Vol. 48, 1894)
The Anti-Marriage League (Blackwood's Magazine, Vol. 159, 1896)

Biographies
Edward Irving (1862)
Francis of Assisi (1871)
Count de Montalembert (1872)
Dante (1877)
Cervantes (1880)
Life of Sheridan in the English Men of Letters series (1883)
John Tulloch (1888)

Laurence Oliphant (1892)

Historical & Critical Works
Historical Sketches of the Reign of George II (1869)
The Makers of Florence (1876)
A Literary History of England from 1760 to 1825 (1882)
The Makers of Venice (1887)
Royal Edinburgh (1890)
Jerusalem (1891)
The Makers of Modern Rome (1895)
William Blackwood and his Sons (1897)
The Sisters Brontë. In: Women Novelists of Queen Victoria's Reign (1897)

www.ingramcontent.com/pod-product-compliance
Lightning Source LLC
Chambersburg PA
CBHW061506170626
46811CB00004B/1628